Life Cycle of a
Butterfly

Angela Royston

Heinemann Library
Des Plaines, Illinois

Designed by Celia Floyd
Illustrations by Alan Fraser
Printed in Hong Kong / China

02 01 00 99
10 9 8 7 6 5 4 3 2

Library of Congress Cataloging-in-Publication Data

Royston, Angela.
    Life cycle of a butterfly / by Angela Royston.
        p.   cm.
    Includes bibliographical references and index.
    Summary: Introduces the life of a Monarch butterfly, from its
beginning as a tiny egg laid on a milkweed leaf through its
metamorphosis from a caterpillar to an adult butterfly.
    ISBN 1-57572-697-1 (lib. bdg.)
    1. Monarch butterfly--Life cycles--Juvenile literature.
[1. Monarch butterfly. 2. Butterflies.] I. Title.
QL561.D3R695   1998
595.78'9--dc21   98-10572
                                                              CIP
                                                              AC

Acknowledgments
The Publisher would like to thank the following for permission to reproduce
photographs:
A–Z Botanical Collection/N. K. D. Miller p. 4; Bruce Coleman/Frans Lanting pp. 26-
27, Bruce Coleman/Andrew J. Purcell p. 18, Bruce Coleman/John Shaw p. 11;
Dembinsky Photo Association/S. Moody p. 10; NHPA/Dr. Eckart Pott pp. 21, 22,
NHPA/John Shaw p. 5, NHPA/Rod Planck p. 12; Oxford Scientific Films/Breck P. Kent
pp. 6, 8, Oxford Scientific Films/J. A. L. Cooke pp. 7, 24, 25, Oxford Scientific
Films/Rudie H. Kuiter pp. 9, 14, 15, 16, 17, Oxford Scientific Films/Tom Ulrich p. 12,
Oxford Scientific Films/Harry Fox p. 19, Oxford Scientific Films/Norbert Wu p. 20,
Oxford Scientific Films/Dan Guravich p. 23.
Cover photograph: Superstock. Our thanks to Anthony M. V. Hoare, Butterfly
Conservation, in the preparation of this edition.

Contents

Meet the Butterflies

A butterfly is an insect. It has six legs, four wings, and two **antennae**. Many butterflies have brightly colored wings, like this swallowtail.

1 day

1 week

4 weeks

6 weeks

Many kinds of butterflies live in different parts of the world. The butterfly in this book is a monarch butterfly from North America.

10 weeks

32 weeks

33 weeks

Eggs Hatching

Every butterfly begins life as a tiny egg. The monarch butterfly lays her eggs on a **milkweed** leaf. Just over a week later, the egg begins to **hatch**.

I day

I week

4 weeks

6 weeks

A small **caterpillar** crawls out of the egg! It ate a hole in the egg and now it will eat the eggshell.

10 weeks

32 weeks

33 weeks

Caterpillar

The **caterpillar** eats and grows bigger. It chews through the leaf with its strong **jaws**. Soon it has eaten a big hole in the **milkweed** leaf.

1 day	1 week	4 weeks	6 weeks

All the eggs have **hatched** and many monarch caterpillars are feeding on the milkweed plant. They crawl from leaf to leaf, eating as they go.

10 weeks

32 weeks

33 weeks

The **caterpillar** grows, but its skin does not. One day its skin is so tight it splits open. The caterpillar has a new and bigger skin underneath!

1 day

1 week

4 weeks

6 weeks

The caterpillar will shed its skin
four times as it grows. Now it
crawls away, clinging to the thin
stem with its many legs.

10 weeks

32 weeks

33 weeks

12

The **caterpillar** eats and grows. It is not eaten by other animals because **milkweed** leaves have something in them that make the caterpillar taste yucky.

I day

I week

4 weeks

6 weeks

This bird catches insects, but when it sees the monarch caterpillar's black and yellow stripes, it leaves it alone. The bird has learned that the monarch tastes yucky.

10 weeks

32 weeks

33 weeks

Pupa

4 weeks

When the **caterpillar** is fully grown it **spins** a silky pad on the bottom of a leaf. It grasps the pad and its striped skin splits for the last time.

1 day

1 week

4 weeks

6 weeks

Underneath the skin is a green **pupa**. The caterpillar is ready to change into a butterfly!

10 weeks

32 weeks

33 weeks

Inside the hard shell of the **pupa**, the **caterpillar's** body changes. Then the pupa cracks open and the butterfly pulls itself free.

16

1 day	1 week	4 weeks	6 weeks

At first its wings are damp and crumpled. As they dry, the wings slowly open. Now the butterfly is ready to fly away.

10 weeks

32 weeks

33 weeks

18

The butterfly flies from flower to flower, feeding on their **nectar**. It unrolls its long tongue and sucks up the sweet juice.

1 day	1 week	4 weeks	6 weeks

Birds do not try to catch the butterfly. The **milkweed** that made the **caterpillar** taste yucky is still in its body, making it taste yucky, too.

10 weeks

32 weeks

33 weeks

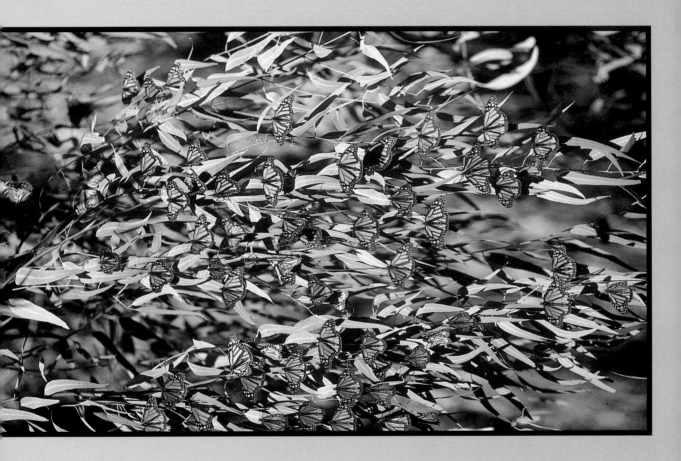

20

It is fall and the weather starts getting cold. The monarch butterflies gather together on the branches of trees.

| 1 day | 1 week | 4 weeks | 6 weeks |

They flutter up into the sky. They fly south until they reach the mountains of Mexico, where the weather is warmer in winter.

10 weeks

32 weeks

33 weeks

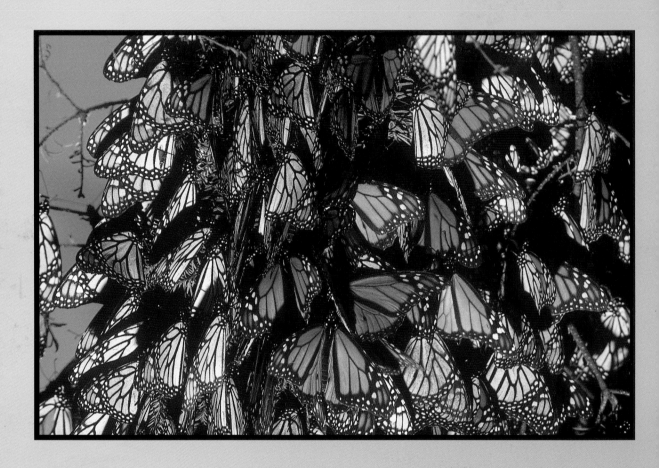

22

The butterflies are very tired. They gather on pine trees to rest and sleep for the winter.

| 1 day | 1 week | 4 weeks | 6 weeks |

In spring the sun warms the butterflies and wakes them up. They feed on **nectar** from flowers. Most of the butterflies start to fly north.

10 weeks

32 weeks

33 weeks

24

The butterflies rest during the journey. This male has found a female that is ready to **mate**. After mating, the female lays her eggs.

I day

I week

4 weeks

6 weeks

She lays them on a **milkweed** plant. The butterflies live only for a few more weeks. By then, new **caterpillars** are **hatching**.

10 weeks

32 weeks

33 weeks

The Journey Continues

Back in Mexico some butterflies have been battered by a big storm. Some recover and will fly north. Others will die along the way.

But along the way, **caterpillars** are **hatching**. When they change into butterflies, they too will fly north. There they will **mate** and lay eggs of their own.

Life Cycle

Eggs Hatching

1

Caterpillar

2

Pupa

3

4
Butterfly

5
Butterfly

Mating

Laying Eggs

6

7

Fact File

The wingspan of a monarch butterfly is nearly as wide as your hand span.

Monarch butterflies fly farther than any other kind of butterfly. During their long journeys north and south they fly up to 1,800 miles (3,000 kilometers.)

Butterflies use their **antennae** to smell and to feel. They smell food and the special smells the male monarch butterfly gives off when he is ready to **mate**.

Glossary

antennae the long, skinny feelers on an insect's head

caterpillar a young butterfly or moth before it changes into a **pupa**

hatch to be born out of an egg

jaws the moving parts of the caterpillar's mouth

mate when a male and a female come together to produce babies

milkweed a kind of plant

nectar the sweet juice produced by some flowers

pupa the stage in life when a **caterpillar** changes into a butterfly

spin to make a long thread

More Books to Read

Crewe, Sabrina. *The Butterfly.* Chatham, NJ: Raintree Steck-Vaughn, 1997.

Heiligman, Deborah. *From Caterpillar to Butterfly.* New York: HarperCollins Children's Books, 1996.

Legg, Gerald. *Caterpillar and Butterfly.* Danbury, CT: Franklin Watts, 1998.

Index